The Big Book of Child Sexual Abuse Awareness

The Ultimate Survival & Healing Guide for Teenagers

Priyanka Verma

DIAMOND BOOKS

www.diamondbooks.in

Publisher : **Diamond Pocket Books (P) Ltd.**
X-30, Okhla Industrial Area, Phase-II
New Delhi-110020
Phone : 011-40712200
E-mail : wecare@diamondbooks.in
Website : www.diamondbooks.in
Edition : 2025
Printed By : Repro (India)

Preface

Child sexual abuse (CSA) is one of the most serious yet often unspoken challenges faced by children and teenagers around the world. It happens in silence, in fear, and often without anyone knowing. As we step into a digital world where online spaces, AI interactions, and social media have become everyday realities for young people, it is more important than ever to equip teens with knowledge, confidence, and tools for their safety and emotional wellbeing.

This book is written for teenagers, with teenagers in mind. It is designed to be simple, honest, and empowering. Whether you're someone who is seeking information, someone trying to heal, or someone who wants to support a friend—you belong here.

We explain what CSA is, how to recognize the signs, how to speak up, how to stay safe (both offline and online), how the law protects you, and how healing is possible.

You will also find:

• Survivor voices
• Journal prompts and affirmations
• Calming tools to help you feel safe again
• Real-life support resources and helplines

This book doesn't believe in scaring you—it believes in powering you. Because you are not alone, and it's never too late to find your voice, your strength, and your path to healing.

With care and courage,

- Priyanka Verma

Foreword

When we talk about the future of our country, we often say, "Children are the future." But to secure that future, we must protect their present. Every child and teenager deserves to grow up in a world where they are safe, heard, and respected. Sadly, many young people face the harsh reality of abuse—often by those they trust the most.

This book is a much-needed guide for today's teens navigating the complexities of body boundaries, consent, digital dangers, and emotional healing. It doesn't just provide facts—it offers hope, language, and support. It helps teenagers understand that they have rights, that it's never their fault, and that help is always available.

As someone working closely with adolescent health and education, I wholeheartedly believe that this resource will change lives. It will help not just survivors, but also parents, teachers, and peers who want to build safer spaces for children.

I urge educators and schools to include this in Life Skills Education, and I encourage every teenager to read this not with fear, but with strength.

Because when teens are informed, they are empowered. And when they are empowered, they are unstoppable.

Contents

Chapter 1

What Is Child Sexual Abuse (CSA)?

Understanding the Basics

Child Sexual Abuse (CSA) is a subject that makes many people uncomfortable. But not talking about it doesn't make it go away. It only allows the abuse to continue in silence. That's why this chapter is here—to help you understand clearly, respectfully, and honestly what CSA is and how to identify it.

At its core, Child Sexual Abuse is any form of sexual activity with a child or teenager that happens without their full understanding, willingness, or legal consent. It can be physical, verbal, emotional, or digital. Abuse is never the fault of the child or teenager—it is always the responsibility of the abuser.

What Is CSA? (The First W)

Sexual abuse involves an imbalance of power. The abuser takes advantage of a child's or teen's trust, innocence, or dependency. It is not just about "bad touch" or "rape." It also includes non-touching abuse, such as showing sexual content, sending explicit messages, or exposing one's body inappropriately.

Examples of CSA:
- Touching a child's private parts without consent
- Forcing or tricking a child to touch someone else's private parts
- Taking or sharing sexual pictures or videos of a minor
- Making a child watch pornography
- Using the internet or social media to send inappropriate content
- Saying sexually explicit things to a child or teenager
- Repeatedly violating a child's personal space in a sexualized way

Why Does It Happen? (The Second W)

It's important to understand that abuse is never the victim's fault. Abuse happens because someone chooses to harm. But why do they do it?

Common reasons behind CSA:
- Power and control: The abuser wants to dominate someone more vulnerable.
- Opportunity and secrecy: Children are often easy to silence or confuse.
- Broken boundaries: The abuser may ignore rules of affection and privacy.
- Digital freedom: Online anonymity makes grooming and exploitation easier.

Many abusers are not strangers. They are often known and trusted—like a relative, teacher, coach, family friend, or neighbor. That's what makes it even more difficult for victims to understand or report what's happening.

When Can CSA Happen? (The Third W)

There is no fixed time or age when CSA might occur. It can happen at any point during childhood or teenage years. Some abuse starts very early, even before the child knows what is happening. Some teenagers face abuse through relationships, threats, or online interactions.

Situations where CSA can occur:
• While staying with a relative or friend
• After school, during tuitions or sports coaching
• At sleepovers or parties without supervision
• In religious spaces, hostels, or schools
• On social media, chatrooms, or gaming platforms

Abuse often happens in private, but it can leave lifelong emotional scars.

Where Can CSA Happen? (The Fourth W)

Contrary to popular belief, CSA doesn't just happen in dark alleys or abandoned buildings. It can happen in places we consider safe and normal.

Common locations:
• At home: Most abuse is by someone the child knows and trusts
• At school or coaching center: Teachers, classmates, or seniors may exploit their position
• Religious or community institutions: Trust and blind faith can sometimes shield predators
• Online platforms: Digital abuse is rising rapidly, through fake identities, video calls, sextortion, and more

That's why children must be taught body boundaries, internet safety, and the power of saying NO—even to someone they know.

Who Can Be Affected by CSA? (The Fifth W)

Anyone can be a victim of CSA. It doesn't matter if you are:

- A boy, girl, or non-binary
- From a city or village
- From a poor or rich background
- Young or in your late teens

Abusers don't target children based on class, gender, or religion. They target based on access, secrecy, and silence.

Also, boys and LGBTQ+ teens often don't report abuse due to fear of judgment or being told "it doesn't happen to boys." But CSA has nothing to do with the victim's gender. It's a crime, plain and simple.

Consent vs. Abuse vs. Affection

This is one of the most misunderstood areas in CSA education. Let's break it down:

What is Consent?

Consent is a clear, voluntary "yes" to a particular action.

It is:

- Freely given
- Informed
- Reversible (can be taken back anytime)
- Enthusiastic
- Specific

A child or teenager cannot give legal consent to sexual activity with an adult. So even if a teen says "yes" under pressure, flattery, or confusion—it is still CSA if the person is older or in a position of power.

What is Abuse?

• It's never okay for anyone to touch your private parts or make you touch theirs
• It's not okay to be touched when you're scared, uncomfortable, confused, or pressured
• It's abuse when someone ignores your NO or silence

What is Healthy Affection?

It's normal to hug, hold hands, or show love in non-sexual, respectful ways.

Examples:
• A parent giving a goodnight kiss
• A sibling giving you a high-five
• A teacher encouraging you with a pat on the back

But if that affection feels weird, secretive, or scary—trust your gut. That "uh-oh" feeling is your body's way of warning you.

The "Uh-oh" Feeling – Your Body's Alarm

You may not always be able to explain it, but if someone:
• Gets too close
• Asks you to keep secrets
• Offers gifts to keep you quiet
• Makes you feel ashamed or weird

...that's a red flag. That "uh-oh" feeling in your stomach or chest means you need to step back and tell someone you trust.

Real-Life Example (Anonymous)

"I was 13. My uncle used to hug me too long, touch me strangely, and say it was a game. I was confused, ashamed, and couldn't tell anyone. One day, I finally told my school counselor. She said, 'It's not your fault.' That sentence changed my life. I wasn't alone anymore."

Checklist: Is This Okay?

Situation	**Okay or Not Okay?**
Uncle hugs you at Diwali and lets go	Okay
Teacher asks you to meet after class in private and touches your back strangely	Not Okay
Friend sends you a sexual image on WhatsApp	Not Okay
Parent gives you a goodnight kiss on the forehead	Okay
Online "friend" asks for your photo in underwear	Not Okay

If you're unsure, talk to a trusted adult. You never have to face this alone.

Journal Prompt:

- What does safety mean to me?
- Who do I trust in my life?
- How does my body feel when I'm safe or unsafe?

Calming Corner Activity:

Deep Breathing:

Breathe in slowly (count to 4), hold (count to 2), breathe out slowly (count to 6).

Repeat 3 times when you feel overwhelmed.

In This Chapter, You Learned:

- The definition and types of CSA
- The 5Ws (What, Why, When, Where, Who)
- The difference between affection, consent, and abuse
- How to trust your inner alarm – the "uh-oh" feeling
- That CSA can happen to anyone—and it's never the victim's fault

Chapter 2

How It Feels

Signs You Shouldn't Ignore

The Invisible Storm

Child Sexual Abuse (CSA) doesn't always leave bruises you can see. Sometimes, the deepest scars are the ones we carry in our hearts and minds. Many teens don't even realize they've been abused because the experience is confusing, hidden behind silence, threats, shame, or mixed emotions. This chapter helps you recognize the emotional, physical, and behavioral signs that something's not right. These signs don't always mean abuse has happened—but they are signals worth listening to. Your mind and body often know the truth before your words do.

Emotional Signs – What the Mind Feels

After experiencing abuse, many teens experience overwhelming emotions—even if they don't fully understand what happened. These feelings can be constant or come and go. They might seem random or sudden. But they are real.

Common Emotional Signs:
• Anxiety – feeling nervous, jumpy, or constantly "on edge"
• Shame or guilt – blaming yourself, feeling "dirty" or "bad"
• Sadness or depression – feeling empty, hopeless, or crying often
• Nightmares or flashbacks – reliving scary moments during sleep or in your mind
• Fear of certain people, places, or being alone
• Confusion – especially if the abuser was someone you liked or trusted

You might find it hard to explain these emotions to others. That's okay. Your feelings are valid, even if you can't fully understand them yet.

Physical Signs – What the Body Shows

While not all abuse involves physical contact, when it does, there can be signs on the body. Unfortunately, many of these are either missed, hidden, or misunderstood.

Watch out for:
• Bruising, swelling, or pain around private areas
• Trouble walking or sitting
• Bleeding or discharge
• Frequent urinary tract infections or stomach pain
• Avoiding medical checkups or feeling ashamed of one's body
• Wearing multiple layers of clothing even when it's hot

Important: These symptoms can also come from other medical conditions. But if they appear suddenly, especially along with emotional changes, they should never be ignored.

Behavioral Signs – How You Act or React

Sometimes, the biggest changes after abuse are in how a person behaves. You may not even realize that your new habits, fears, or moods are linked to what happened. That's why it's so important to pause and reflect.

Some behavior changes to notice:
- Withdrawing from family or friends
- Sudden anger or aggression
- Constant fear or silence
- Running away from home or school
- A drop in academic performance
- Loss of interest in activities you once enjoyed
- Using alcohol, cigarettes, or drugs to cope
- Becoming overly sexualized in speech or behavior
- Self-harm or hurting oneself

The "Uh-oh" Feeling – Trust Your Gut

Our brains have an in-built alarm system. When someone makes you feel unsafe—even without touching you—your gut often sends signals.

You might feel:
- A tight chest
- A knot in your stomach
- Nausea or chills
- A racing heart
- A feeling of "I want to get out of here"

This is your body's way of saying: "Something's wrong." Don't ignore it. You don't need proof to feel what you feel.

Real Voices – Survivor Quotes

"I didn't know what he did was wrong. I just knew I didn't like it and felt scared when he came close. But I couldn't tell anyone. I thought I'd be blamed."

— Anonymous, 15 years old

"I kept crying without knowing why. I was angry all the time. Only in therapy did I learn that my body was holding on to the fear I never spoke about."

— Survivor, 17 years old

These stories reflect a sad truth: many teens keep silent because they don't recognize abuse or feel they won't be believed.

Why Some Teens Don't Speak Up

Even if a teenager senses something wrong, they may not report it.

Here's why:
- Fear of not being believed
- Fear of punishment or shame
- Love for the abuser (often a relative)
- Confusion about consent or touch
- Not knowing what happened was abuse
- Cultural silence or stigma

Abusers often manipulate their victims with lines like:
- "This is our little secret."
- "No one will believe you."
- "You'll break the family if you talk."

But here's the truth: Speaking up breaks silence, not families. Speaking up saves lives.

Common Myths vs. Facts

Myth	Reality
"Only girls are abused."	Boys and LGBTQ+ teens are also abused, often silently.
"If there's no mark, there's no abuse."	Most abuse leaves emotional, not visible scars.
"If it felt confusing, maybe it wasn't abuse."	Abuse is often confusing. That doesn't make it okay.
"You didn't say no, so maybe you agreed."	Silence is not consent. Fear freezes people.
"You're overreacting."	No reaction to abuse is ever "too much." Your pain is valid.

Safety Check: Am I Okay?

If you feel "off" and wonder if it's linked to something unsafe, ask yourself:

- Do I feel scared around a particular person?
- Do I avoid places where someone touches or stares at me strangely?
- Do I get anxious, have bad dreams, or want to run away?
- Have I changed how I dress, act, or feel to avoid someone?
- Do I have feelings of guilt, confusion, or anger I can't explain?

If you answered "yes" to any of these—pause. Reflect. Speak to someone you trust. These signs are your body and mind asking for help.

What You Can Do

- Talk to someone – a parent, school counselor, helpline, teacher, or friend
- Write your feelings in a private journal

• Reach out for therapy – it doesn't mean you're "weak"; it means you're healing
• Use grounding tools to stay calm (see next section)
• Believe your own feelings – even if others doubt them

Calming Corner: Grounding Technique

The 5-4-3-2-1 Rule

When overwhelmed, do this:
• 5 things you can see
• 4 things you can touch
• 3 things you can hear
• 2 things you can smell
• 1 thing you can taste

This brings your brain back to the present—a safe space.

My Journal Space

• "The last time I felt unsafe was…"
• "When I'm scared, I want to…"
• "If I had a magical safety shield, it would do…"

Summary

In this chapter, you learned:
• The emotional, physical, and behavioral signs of CSA
• That abuse often causes silence, confusion, and shame
• That your gut instincts are important and should not be ignored
• That even if you don't fully understand what happened—you deserve help and healing

Chapter 3

Grooming

The Hidden Danger

What Is Grooming?

When we think of abuse, we often imagine a sudden act of violence or inappropriate touch. But many times, it doesn't start like that. It begins with something subtle, friendly—even caring. That's called grooming.

Grooming is a process where an abuser builds a relationship, trust, and emotional connection with a young person so they can exploit, manipulate, or abuse them later.

Grooming is slow, sneaky, and confusing. It's designed to break your guard and make you feel guilty or responsible. It's not about love—it's about control.

Why Grooming Works

The truth is: most abusers aren't strangers. They're someone known, someone trusted. They may act like a friend, a relative, a mentor, or a romantic partner. They may give compliments, offer help, or listen to your problems—all with a hidden motive.

Abusers groom to:
• Make the child feel "special"
• Create a secret bond
• Slowly cross personal boundaries
• Make the victim doubt themselves
• Ensure silence through guilt or fear

Stages of Grooming

Let's break it down. Grooming usually follows these 5 stages:
1. Targeting the Victim
The abuser looks for someone who:
• Seems lonely, insecure, or in need of attention
• Is emotionally vulnerable
• Has access (neighbor, student, relative, friend's child)
• Has limited adult supervision

2. Gaining Trust
The abuser may:
• Offer gifts or treats
• Listen with unusual interest
• Compliment constantly
• Join activities you enjoy
• Act protective or caring
This phase often feels flattering. You might think, "Wow, someone finally understands me."

3. Building Emotional Dependency
The abuser creates a space where:
• You rely on them emotionally
• You share secrets with them
• You feel "loved," "understood," or even "indebted"

• They might say: "No one else gets you like I do."
This is a trap of emotional control.

4. Isolating the Victim

The abuser might:

• Say your parents or friends "don't get you"
• Encourage you to keep things secret
• Discourage you from spending time with others
• Make you feel guilty for talking to someone else

They start cutting off your safety net.

5. Abuse and Maintaining Control

Once trust is built, they might:

• Touch you inappropriately
• Ask for sexual favors or photos
• Threaten to expose your secrets if you speak up
• Say, "You asked for it," "You liked it," or "You'll ruin everything"

This stage is where the abuse becomes clear—but the manipulation often keeps the victim silent.

Examples of Grooming Behavior

What It Looks Like	Why It's Dangerous
Sending constant compliments like "You're so mature for your age"	Creates false emotional intimacy
Giving secret gifts or money	Builds guilt and secrecy
Asking to keep conversations hidden	Breaks safe boundaries
Asking for pictures or sending selfies	Normalizes sexual exchange
Saying "No one will understand us"	Isolates you from support
Inviting you for private meetups	Increases risk of abuse

Online Grooming – The New Playground

Today, grooming is not just physical—it's digital. With social media, chats, games, and video platforms,

Grooming can happen through:

- Instagram DMs
- Online gaming platforms
- WhatsApp or Signal
- Dating or anonymous chat apps
- Live streaming platforms

Abusers create fake profiles pretending to be:

- Your age
- A supportive adult
- A talent scout or modeling agent
- A "fan" or "admirer"

They send compliments, flirty messages, or photos—and slowly ask for the same in return.

This is still grooming, even if it happens online.

AI & Deepfake Risks

Technology has added a dark layer to grooming. Today, abusers may:

- Use AI tools to create fake identities
- Use your selfies to create deepfake videos or images
- Threaten to "leak" personal chats or photos unless you give in

These are forms of sextortion—a digital abuse crime. It's scary, but you're not helpless. You can:

- Block and report the user
- Inform a trusted adult
- Report to cybercrime portals
- Never give in to blackmail

Safe vs. Unsafe Secrets

Not all secrets are bad—but some are unhealthy and dangerous.

Safe Secret	Unsafe Secret
Planning a surprise birthday party	Someone asks you to hide inappropriate texts or photos
Keeping a fun joke between friends	Someone says "don't tell anyone, or you'll be in trouble"
Keeping your diary private	Someone makes you feel scared or ashamed if you share the secret

Rule: If a secret makes you feel confused, scared, or ashamed—tell a trusted adult immediately.

What Grooming Is Not:

• It's not "just being friendly"
• It's not "flirting between equals"
• It's not "mentorship" when boundaries are crossed
• It's not "your fault"

Even if you didn't say "no" or even if you liked the attention at first—grooming is never okay. You were being manipulated.

Real Voice – A Survivor's Story

"He was my neighbor. He used to help me with homework. I trusted him. He started texting me late at night, sending heart emojis, saying I was beautiful. Then he asked for pictures. When I said no, he said he'd tell my parents I was 'asking for it.' I was only 14. I blocked him and told my teacher. That saved me."
— Anonymous Teen Survivor

What To Do If You Suspect Grooming

If someone is:

- Making you feel special in secretive ways
- Crossing your personal boundaries
- Making you emotionally dependent on them
- Asking for things that make you uncomfortable

You must:

Tell a trusted adult (parent, teacher, counselor)
Block and report the person on all platforms
Save screenshots or messages for evidence
Call 1098 CHILDLINE or a helpline
Know you did nothing wrong

Calming Corner: "Shield Visualization"

Close your eyes. Imagine a glowing shield around you.
It blocks anything unsafe—words, touches, threats.
Breathe in strength. Breathe out fear.
Repeat: "I am allowed to say NO. I am worth protecting."

My Journal Space

- Who are the people I trust in my life?
- What makes me feel emotionally safe?
- Have I ever kept a secret that made me uncomfortable?

Summary

In this chapter, you learned:

- Grooming is manipulation, not affection
- It can happen slowly—offline or online
- Abusers use secrets, guilt, flattery, and isolation
- Safe relationships never ask you to hide, lie, or fear
- You can break the grooming cycle by trusting your gut and asking for help

Chapter 4

How Abuse Impacts the Brain & Heart

What Is Trauma?

When someone goes through something terrifying—like sexual abuse—the body and brain react in powerful ways. Even when the abuse ends, the fear, confusion, and pain can stay inside, like an emotional storm that refuses to calm.

That storm is called trauma.
Trauma is not just what happened to you. It's how your mind and body react to what happened—especially when it was unexpected, scary, confusing, and not your fault.
Sexual abuse, especially in childhood or teenage years, can leave a

lasting impact on:

- The brain's ability to feel safe
- The heart's ability to trust
- The body's ability to relax and heal

But here's the good news: Healing is possible. First, let's understand what's happening inside you.

What Happens in the Brain During Trauma?

When something dangerous or confusing happens, your brain switches to survival mode. The part of your brain that handles logic takes a back seat.

Instead, your brain says:
"Am I in danger? What do I do to survive?"

That's when you might:
• Freeze (become still and numb)
• Fight (lash out or yell)
• Flight (run away or avoid)
• Fawn (try to please the abuser to stay safe)

These are not choices. They are automatic reactions from your nervous system. Your brain is just trying to protect you.

Common Emotional Effects After CSA

After abuse, teens often struggle with emotional turbulence. These feelings are valid, even if you can't explain them clearly.

Some common emotional reactions include:
• **Depression:** Deep sadness, emptiness, loss of joy
• **Anxiety:** Constant worry, racing thoughts, tight chest
• **Shame:** Feeling "dirty" or "to blame" (even though you're not)
• **Guilt:** Thinking "I should've stopped it" (you couldn't, and that's okay)
• **Anger or rage:** At the abuser, yourself, or even others
• **Loneliness:** Feeling like no one would understand

Feeling "Not Real" – What Is Dissociation?

Some teens report a strange feeling of disconnect after trauma. You might:

- Feel like you're outside your body
- Have memory blanks
- "Numb out" during certain times
- Zone out in class or while talking

This is called dissociation. It's your mind's way of protecting itself when something is too much to handle.
It's common after CSA—and it's not your fault. You're not broken. You're protecting yourself.

How Trauma Affects the Body

Even when the abuse stops, the body remembers. Trauma often leads to physical symptoms,

such as:

- Headaches, stomach aches, fatigue
- Sleep problems (insomnia, nightmares)
- Changes in appetite
- Feeling dizzy, shaky, or weak

- **Panic attacks:** shortness of breath, heart racing, sweating

These aren't "just in your head." They're real symptoms of emotional pain.

Why You Might Struggle with School or Friends

Trauma can affect how you:

- Trust others
- Focus in class
- Express emotions

• Handle relationships
• React to jokes or physical touch

You might pull away from friends or become overly dependent. You might fear being judged, touched, or misunderstood.
That's not weakness. That's a sign you need care—not criticism.

Trauma and Self-Harm

Some teens try to cope with pain by:
• Cutting themselves
• Burning or hitting themselves
• Refusing food
• Abusing substances
They do this not for attention, but to release emotional pain, feel in control, or feel something when they feel numb.

If this is you—please know:
• You are not alone
• You are not "crazy"
• You deserve support, not shame
There are healthier ways to feel safe again—and help is available.

Understanding PTSD (Post-Traumatic Stress Disorder)

Not everyone who experiences CSA develops PTSD, but many do.
Signs of PTSD:
• **Flashbacks:** feeling like the abuse is happening again
• **Avoidance:** staying away from people, places, or topics
• **Hypervigilance:** always on edge, startled easily
• **Numbness:** feeling nothing, even when you want to
• Emotional outbursts or breakdowns
PTSD is not a label for life—it's a response to deep pain, and it can improve with the right help.

You Are Not to Blame – Ever

Repeat after us:
"I didn't invite it. I didn't want it. I didn't cause it. I don't deserve the blame."
CSA is a crime, and the responsibility lies 100% with the abuser. Your silence, confusion, or compliance under pressure doesn't make you guilty. It makes you a survivor.

Real Voices – Healing Is Possible

"For a long time, I felt broken. I hated my body. I didn't trust anyone. But therapy taught me it wasn't my fault. Now, I'm reclaiming who I am."— Teen Survivor, Age 17
"I had panic attacks whenever someone hugged me. I used to think I was weak. But now I know I was just wounded. And wounds can heal."— Anonymous, 16

Calming Corner: Grounding With the Body

When your trauma takes over, try this grounding tool:
"Feel Your Feet" Technique:
- Stand still
- Notice your feet touching the ground
- Press your heels down slowly
- Wiggle your toes
- **Say:** "I am safe. I am here. I am now."

This brings your body back to the present when anxiety takes you back to the past.

My Journal Space

- What does "being safe" mean to me?
- When do I feel calm or in control?
- What helps me feel stronger inside?

Coping Kit: Things That Help

- Drawing or coloring your feelings
- Talking to a school counselor
- Listening to calming music
- Using a weighted blanket or soft toy
- Practicing deep breathing
- Spending time in nature

Everyone's healing path is different. You get to find what works for you.

Checklist: Do I Need Help?

If you say yes to two or more of these, it's time to reach out:

I often feel scared, sad, or angry without knowing why
I avoid people or places linked to my past
I feel "blank" or not present
I've had thoughts of hurting myself
I'm having trouble sleeping, eating, or focusing
I feel like I'll never be okay again
Help is not weakness. It's strength in action.

Summary

In this chapter, you learned:

- What trauma is and how the brain reacts to abuse
- That emotional and physical symptoms are valid
- About PTSD, dissociation, and coping struggles
- That self-blame is misplaced—you did nothing wrong
- That healing is not only possible—it's deserved

Chapter 5

Telling Someone

Breaking the Silence

Why It's Hard to Speak Up

One of the biggest hurdles a teenager faces after experiencing child sexual abuse (CSA) is telling someone.

There are many reasons why speaking up feels terrifying:
• "What if they don't believe me?"
• "What if they blame me?"
• "What if it ruins my family?"
• "What if I'm overreacting?"
• "What if I can't explain what happened?"

These are real fears. But here's something just as real:
Silence protects the abuser. Speaking up protects you.
Breaking the silence is the first brave step toward healing, justice, and freedom.

Why Do Teens Stay Silent?

Let's understand the silence—not judge it.

Common reasons teens stay silent:
• The abuser is someone they love or trust
• They were told it's "just a game" or "nothing serious"
• They fear being blamed or punished
• They don't have the words to describe what happened
• Cultural taboos around sex and modesty
• They fear disrupting the family or hurting a parent
• They were threatened to stay quiet

But the truth is:
Your silence isn't protection. It's a burden you weren't meant to carry alone.

Who Can You Talk To?

Choosing the right person matters. You need someone who:
• Listens without judgment
• Takes you seriously
• Puts your safety first
• Doesn't try to cover it up

Trusted adults can include:
• Parents or guardians
• Older siblings
• School counselor or principal
• Teacher or coach
• Relative you trust
• Doctor or psychologist
• NGO worker or child rights officer
If the first person doesn't believe you, try another. Keep going until someone hears you.

How to Tell – A Simple Script

You don't need to have perfect words. You just need to start.

Try saying:

• "I need to tell you something important. It's hard, but I need your help."
• "Someone did something to me that made me feel scared and uncomfortable."
• "This person [name if you feel safe] touched me in a way that didn't feel right."
• "I've been keeping a secret because I was scared. But I can't anymore."
• "Can we talk privately? I need you to listen and believe me."

You can also write a letter, send a text, or draw what happened if talking is too hard.

What Happens After You Tell?

What you say can set things in motion. Here's what to expect:

If you tell a responsible adult:

• They may comfort you and tell you it's not your fault
• They may talk to other family members or professionals
• They might report the abuse to authorities or school authorities
• They will likely help you get counseling or support

If they don't react the way they should, don't let that stop you. The problem is with them, not you.

Real Reactions – What Teens Said

"I told my mom. She froze. Then she cried. Then she hugged me. I was scared at first, but in that hug, I finally felt safe."
— Ria, 16
"I told my teacher by writing her a letter. She passed it to the

counselor. I was terrified, but now I'm in therapy and it's helping."
— Anonymous, 15
"I told my uncle what my cousin did. He said I was lying. That hurt more than the abuse. But then my aunt stepped in. She believed me. She helped me find my voice again."
— R, 17

What If They Don't Believe You?

Unfortunately, some people:
- Deny what happened
- Defend the abuser
- Say things like "Are you sure?" or "Don't make trouble"

If that happens:
- You are STILL right to speak up
- You did NOT imagine it
- Try again with a different trusted adult
- Contact a helpline or NGO directly

Silence helps no one. Speaking up might take more than one try—but it's worth it.

What to Expect Emotionally After Disclosing

After telling someone, you may feel:
- Relieved
- Scared
- Ashamed
- Confused
- Proud
- Angry

All of these are valid. It's okay to have mixed emotions.
Give yourself time. You've done something incredibly brave.

Calming Corner: The "Courage Hand"

Draw your hand on paper. On each finger, write:
- A person who supports me
- A place I feel safe
- A word that gives me courage
- A thing I love about myself
- A step I've taken toward healing

This becomes your reminder of bravery.

My Journal Space

- Who do I want to tell and why?
- What would I say if I felt safe?
- What does safety feel like to me?

Affirmation Wall

Say these out loud or write them where you can see them:
- "I deserve to be safe."
- "It's okay to speak up."
- "It's not my fault."
- "I am brave for telling."
- "My voice matters."

Helplines You Can Contact (India)

- CHILDLINE 1098 – 24/7 free, confidential help
- iCall – 9152987821 (Mental health support)
- Aarambh India – www.aarambhindia.org
- RAHI Foundation, Arpan, Sakshi – Support organizations for survivors
- Cyber Crime Reporting – www.cybercrime.gov.in

You're not alone. Help is out there. Right now.

Summary

In this chapter, you learned:

- How to safely tell a trusted adult
- What to expect after disclosing abuse
- What to do if you're not believed
- That telling your story is not weakness—it's courage in action

Chapter 6

Getting Help

You're Not Alone

The First Step: Reaching Out

After experiencing or witnessing child sexual abuse (CSA), one of the most important realizations is this: You don't have to go through it alone.

Help is not just a phone number or a website. Help is a lifeline—a teacher who listens, a counselor who understands, a support group that says, "We believe you."

Getting help is not about weakness. It's about survival, healing, and reclaiming your life.

Why Professional Help Matters

Talking to friends is helpful. But professionals—counselors, therapists, psychologists—**are trained to help survivors:**

- Understand what happened
- Work through fear, guilt, and trauma

- Rebuild trust and confidence
- Learn coping strategies
- Start the journey of emotional healing

You don't need to "get over it" alone. You need to work through it with the right support.

What Is Therapy?

Therapy is a safe, private space where you can talk about your feelings, experiences, fears, and thoughts without judgment.

You might talk to:

- A school counselor
- A child psychologist
- A social worker from an NGO
- A trauma therapist

You don't need a diagnosis or label. Just your truth. Therapy helps you understand your own story—and move forward.

What Happens in Therapy?

In a typical session, you might:

- Talk about what happened (only when you're ready)
- Explore how it made you feel
- Learn how to manage panic, sadness, or anger
- Use art, drawing, or journaling if words are hard
- Practice calming tools like breathing or grounding

Everything is private, unless you are in danger. Therapists are there to support, not judge.

Survivor Voice

"I didn't want to go to therapy. I thought it meant I was broken. But my therapist helped me feel human again. I laughed. I cried. I learned that I could be strong and soft. That was healing."
— Teen Survivor, 16

Where Can You Get Help?

In Your School:
- School counselor or mental health coordinator
- Trusted teacher or principal
- Anti-bullying or protection officer

In Your Community:
- Child welfare NGOs
- District Child Protection Unit
- Hospitals with adolescent mental health services

National Helplines (India):
- CHILDLINE 1098 – 24/7 for children in distress
- iCall – 9152987821 – Confidential mental health support
- Aarambh India – Legal and emotional support
- Cybercrime Portal – www.cybercrime.gov.in – For online abuse

The Role of POCSO Act (India)

If you report the abuse, here's what the POCSO Act (Protection of **Children from Sexual Offences) provides:**
- Your identity is protected
- Child-friendly police procedures
- Confidential court trials
- Access to free legal aid
- Right to therapy and counseling

You have rights. You are protected by law.

How Trusted Adults Can Support You

If you're a parent, teacher, or adult reading this, here's how you can help a teen survivor:

- Believe them
- Don't ask "Why didn't you tell earlier?"
- Avoid blaming, questioning, or panicking
- Focus on their safety and feelings
- Help them access therapy and legal support
- Offer calm, unconditional love

Your response can either heal or harm. Choose support.

Calming Corner: The "Safety Bubble" Technique

Close your eyes.
Imagine a glowing bubble around you.
It blocks all fear, shame, or threats.
Inside your bubble, you are protected.
Breathe in safety. Breathe out fear.
Repeat: "I am healing. I am protected. I am not alone."

My Journal Space

- When I feel scared, what helps me calm down?
- Who are three people I trust right now?
- If I could say anything to someone who hurt me, what would it be?

Coping Tools That Help

Tool	How It Helps
Talking to a counselor	Releases emotional weight
Breathing exercises	Reduces anxiety
Drawing or painting	Expresses feelings without words
Journaling	Makes emotions clearer

Music or dance	Releases energy and stress
Group support	Shows you're not alone

Try what feels right. Healing isn't one-size-fits-all.

You Deserve Help Even If…

- It happened years ago
- You didn't tell anyone before
- You're not sure what exactly happened
- You were scared or confused during it
- The person who hurt you is "respected" or "loved" by others

Abuse is still abuse. You are still worthy of help, healing, and justice.

Real Voices – From Pain to Power

"I joined a survivor circle at a local NGO. At first, I couldn't speak. Just sat and cried. But being in a room where no one judged me—where everyone got it—was the beginning of my healing."
— Ayesha, 17
"I called 1098 just to ask questions. I didn't even say my name. But they listened. They helped me breathe. That day, I didn't feel invisible."
— Anonymous Boy, 15

Emergency Safety Plan

If you ever feel unsafe:
1. Find a safe adult or space (school, friend's house, police station)
2. Call 1098 or emergency services
3. Keep a safety contact list (name, number, location)
4. Use code words with trusted friends ("Call me" = I need help)
5. Don't wait. Act immediately.

Your safety comes first. Always.

Summary

In this chapter, you learned:

- That professional help is essential and available
- Where and how to access support (school, NGOs, helplines)
- That the POCSO Act protects your rights
- That you are not alone, and healing is possible
- That support comes in many forms—therapy, journaling, friends, law.

Chapter 7

Safety in a Digital World

Welcome to the Digital Age

You live in a world of smartphones, DMs, video calls, and anonymous apps. The internet is amazing—it helps you learn, connect, express, and have fun. But like every powerful tool, it comes with risks.

Today, child sexual abuse doesn't just happen in person. It happens online—in games, chatrooms, social media, video calls, and even through AI-generated fake identities.
This chapter is about protecting your digital self: your photos, your chats, your body, and your mind.

What Is Online Sexual Abuse?

Online sexual abuse is when someone uses the internet to:
- Share or demand sexual content
- Send sexual messages or images

• Force or trick someone into video calls or acts
• Threaten, blackmail, or stalk online
This abuse is just as serious as physical abuse—and often harder to detect.

Sextortion: A Real Threat

Sextortion is when someone uses threats or blackmail to get sexual photos, videos, or favors from a person.

It usually starts like this:
1. A stranger (or someone you know) compliments you.
2. They ask for a picture or start a flirty chat.
3. You feel special, wanted, or curious—and maybe you send something.
4. Suddenly, they turn threatening:
  o "Send more or I'll post this."
  o "Give me what I want or I'll tell your parents."

This is a crime, and you are not to blame.

Common Platforms for Abuse

Online predators use:
• Instagram, Snapchat, WhatsApp
• Online games with chat features (PUBG, Free Fire, etc.)
• Anonymous Q&A or chat apps
• Telegram and Discord groups
• Fake job offers or modeling auditions

Sometimes they pose as:
• Someone your age
• A fan or follower
• A talent scout or influencer
• A lonely teen "just like you"

Red Flags – What to Watch Out For

If someone:

- Asks for photos of your body
- Tries to move the conversation from public to private chat
- Insists on secrecy
- Sends inappropriate content
- Makes you feel uncomfortable, even slightly
- Keeps asking "Do you trust me?" or "Show me more"

STOP. BLOCK. TELL someone.

AI & Deepfake Dangers

We now live in a time where technology can create fake realities. Dangers include:

- Fake AI profiles (photos that look real but aren't)
- Deepfake videos using your face or voice
- AI bots chatting with you in human-like ways
- Generating fake romantic or sexual conversations

You may be talking to a machine or predator. If it feels "off," trust your gut.

Digital Safety Tips

Do	**Don't**
Keep profiles private	Share passwords with anyone
Use strong passwords	Click unknown links
Block/report strange DMs	Send private pictures/videos
Turn off location tags	Accept friend requests from strangers
Use 2-step verification	Join shady groups or secret chats

"Think Before You Click" Checklist

Ask yourself before posting or sending:
- Would I be okay if a teacher saw this?
- Could someone misuse this?
- Does this make me uncomfortable?
- Is this something I'll regret later?
- Do I trust this person with my privacy?

If the answer is no or maybe, don't send or share.

How to Report Online Abuse

If you are being harassed, blackmailed, or threatened online:
1. Do NOT respond further
2. Take screenshots
3. Block the person
4. Tell a trusted adult
5. **Report at:** www.cybercrime.gov.in
6. Call 1098 or contact a child protection NGO

You can report anonymously.

Real Voices – What Teens Faced

"He was nice at first. Then he started asking for photos. When I refused, he threatened me. I was terrified. But I told my cousin. We reported him. I blocked him, and I got help."
— Anonymous, 16

"Someone created a fake profile with my pics. I felt sick. I cried for days. But my school counselor helped me file a report. Now I know how to keep my settings safe."
— Anonymous Girl, 15

Calming Corner: Screen Detox Moment

Try this once a day:

- Turn off your phone for 10 minutes
- Close your eyes
- Breathe in and out slowly
- **Say:** "I control my screen. My screen does not control me."

Digital calm = mental strength.

My Journal Space

- How does social media make me feel?
- Who online makes me feel safe or unsafe?
- What boundaries do I want to set for myself?

Tech Tools for Safety

- Google Family Link – monitors app usage
- SafeToNet – filters risky messages
- ReThink App – alerts before sending risky texts
- Cybercrime Portal (India) – report abuse
- Instagram & WhatsApp Tools – block/report/filter content

Use tech to protect—not harm—yourself.

Build Your Digital Boundary Rules

Create a personal code:

1. I won't talk to strangers online.
2. I won't send personal photos to anyone.
3. I'll trust my gut if something feels weird.
4. I will tell a trusted adult if I feel unsafe.
5. I will block and report, not freeze.

You deserve digital freedom with protection.

Summary

In this chapter, you learned:

- What online abuse and sextortion look like
- How predators use chats, games, and fake identities
- That AI and deepfake tech can also be dangerous
- How to stay safe, block, report, and protect your digital self
- That your safety matters more than likes or followers

Chapter 8

Healing After Abuse

Yes, It's Possible

Healing Is Not a Straight Line

You've been through something incredibly difficult. Maybe it feels like your world turned upside down. Maybe you feel lost, broken, or numb.

But here's the truth:

You can heal.

You are not broken.

You are not defined by what happened to you.

Healing is not quick. It's not perfect. But it's possible, and it starts with one brave step at a time.

Common Feelings Survivors Have

After child sexual abuse (CSA), teens often go through a swirl of emotions. All of these feelings are normal. They don't make you weak—they make you human.

You might feel:

- Ashamed or dirty
- Guilty, like you caused it (you didn't)
- Scared or panicky, even in safe places
- Numb or disconnected from your body
- Angry or full of rage
- Lonely or misunderstood
- Hopeless, like you'll never feel normal again

The good news? None of these feelings are permanent.

Healing Emotionally – What It Looks Like

Emotional healing is not about forgetting. It's about:

- Making peace with the past
- Reclaiming your self-worth
- Learning to feel safe in your own body
- Finding joy and purpose again

Healing might include:

- Talking to a therapist
- Crying (a lot)
- Setting boundaries
- Feeling all your emotions without guilt
- Learning grounding and self-care tools
- Celebrating your progress—big or small

You get to decide your healing path. There is no right or wrong way.

Expression Heals

Words can heal. So can color, music, and movement.

Try:

- **Journaling:** Write how you feel without censoring yourself.
- **Drawing or painting:** Express emotions without needing words.
- **Dancing or movement:** Release trauma stored in the body.

• **Music:** Make playlists for every mood—sadness, strength, hope.
• **Voice notes to self:** Record messages like, "I'm proud of you."
These are not silly activities. They're healing tools.

Journaling Prompts

• "Today, I feel…"
• "My body feels…"
• "What I wish someone told me after the abuse…"
• "I am learning that I deserve…"
• "If I could talk to my younger self, I would say…"
Try journaling without judgment. This is just for you.

From Survivor to Thriver

Survivors are not just people who "got through it." They are people who:
• Found strength in their truth
• Rebuilt their identity
• Learned to trust again
• Became warriors of hope

You don't have to be fearless to heal.
You just have to keep showing up for yourself.

Real Survivor Stories

"I blamed myself for two years. Then I went to therapy. My therapist helped me realize I was a child, and he was an adult who abused power. Now I run support circles for others."
— **Megha, 18**
"Every time I had a flashback, I thought I was broken. But I learned to breathe, name my emotions, and use grounding. I'm still healing, but I finally feel free in my own body again."
— **Anonymous Boy, 17**

Calming Corner: Butterfly Hug Technique

This gentle technique helps soothe anxiety and re-ground your body.

Steps:
1. Cross your arms over your chest like a butterfly.
2. Tap your shoulders lightly, left–right–left–right.
3. Breathe deeply. Imagine wings wrapping around you.
4. Repeat slowly for 1–2 minutes.

Say to yourself:
"I am safe. I am healing. I am here."

What If You Relapse Emotionally?

Some days, you'll feel strong. Other days, a memory, smell, or place might trigger old pain.
This doesn't mean you're back to square one.
It means you're processing deeply, and that takes time.

When you feel overwhelmed:
- Take deep breaths
- Reach out to your therapist or trusted adult
- Use grounding tools (touch something cold, name objects you see)
- **Remind yourself:** "This is a memory. Not a current danger."

Healing is not a race. Be gentle with yourself.

Understanding Flashbacks

Flashbacks feel like reliving the abuse. They can come through:
- Nightmares
- Sudden body sensations
- Smells, sounds, or places
- Emotional flooding

You are not "crazy." Flashbacks are a normal trauma response. With practice and therapy, you can manage them better.

Affirmations for Healing

Say these aloud or write them down:
- "I am more than what happened to me."
- "My voice matters."
- "My body is mine."
- "Healing is messy—and that's okay."
- "I deserve peace, love, and safety."
- "I am proud of myself for surviving."

Even if you don't believe them yet—keep saying them. Belief will come.

Finding Hope in the Future

You can:
- Fall in love
- Laugh again
- Go to college
- Build healthy relationships
- Help others
- Start a career
- Dance at your best friend's wedding
- Feel at home in your body again

You are not limited by your trauma.
You are being reborn from it.

Personal Healing Plan

Take a blank page and answer:
1. What does healing mean to me?
2. What support do I need right now?

3. What makes me feel safe?
4. What are three things I enjoy?
5. What helps me feel calm when I'm stressed?
6. One goal for next week:
7. One word I want to hold onto:

Keep this as your healing roadmap.

Summary

In this chapter, you learned:

- That healing is possible, even if it feels far away
- How to use journaling, art, breathing, and affirmations as tools
- That survivor stories are full of resilience and courage
- That healing is not perfect—it's progress
- That you are worthy of safety, love, and joy

Chapter 9

If It Happened to a Friend

When a Friend Tells You Something Deeply Personal

Imagine this: A friend looks you in the eye and says, "I need to tell you something... something bad happened to me."
Your heart pounds. You freeze. You may not know what to say.

But here's the truth: Just being there is powerful.
If a friend opens up about child sexual abuse (CSA), it means they trust you deeply. Your response can help them feel supported—or shut down completely.

This chapter is about how to:
- Listen with empathy
- Respond safely
- Avoid judgment
- Encourage healing

First, Breathe. Then Listen.

You may feel shocked, angry, or even confused. That's normal. But your friend needs you to be calm, kind, and steady.

Here's what you can do in the moment:

DO:
- Pause. Breathe. Listen.
- Make eye contact, nod, stay present
- Speak slowly and gently
- Keep your phone away—give full attention

DON'T:
- Interrupt or ask for graphic details
- Act shocked or horrified
- Question their memory or timing
- Talk about your own problems

Right now, this moment is about them.

What to Say

Sometimes it's hard to find the right words. Here are some simple,

powerful responses:
- "I believe you."
- "I'm so sorry this happened to you."
- "It's not your fault."
- "Thank you for trusting me."
- "I'm here for you."

You don't need to "fix" it.
You just need to show up with your heart.

What Not to Say

Even with good intentions, some phrases can hurt more than help.

Avoid saying:
• "Are you sure?"
• "Why didn't you tell anyone earlier?"
• "What were you wearing?"
• "You should've stopped them."
• "Don't tell anyone—you'll get them in trouble."
• "That's too heavy for me."

These statements cause shame, doubt, and silence.
Replace judgment with kindness.

Why They Told You (and Not Someone Else)

It's not that you're the only person they trust—but you might be the one who:
• Listens without gossiping
• Respects feelings without overreacting
• Has shown empathy in small ways before
• Feels "safe" even in silence

Don't dismiss your importance.
To them, you are a lifeline.

What Should You Do Next?

Supporting your friend doesn't mean doing it all alone.

Here's a gentle plan:
1. **Reassure them:** "You're not alone."
2. **Ask gently:** "Do you want help finding someone to talk to?"
3. **Offer options, not pressure:** "Would you like to speak to a school

counselor or adult together?"
4. Let them lead their own healing timeline.
5. Respect their privacy—but report if their safety is at risk.

If they're in immediate danger or the abuse is ongoing, you must tell a trusted adult or call CHILDLINE 1098.

What If You're the Only One Who Knows?

This can feel overwhelming. But silence can keep them unsafe.

If your friend:

- Is being abused right now
- Is thinking of self-harm
- Is too scared to speak up

Then it is okay—and necessary—to report it to a school counselor, parent, or authority, even without their permission.
You're not betraying them.
You're protecting their life.

Real Voices – What Helped

"I told my best friend first. She didn't say much. Just held my hand. That's all I needed."
— Anonymous, 15

"My friend told our school counselor because I was too scared. At first I was mad. But later I thanked him. That saved me."
— Survivor, 17

"All I wanted was someone to sit next to me without asking questions. My friend did that. She made me feel real again."
— Riya, 16

Calming Corner: Supportive Breathing for Two

If your friend is panicking or crying, try this:
1. Sit beside them, shoulder to shoulder.
2. Breathe in slowly (4 seconds), hold (2), exhale (6).
3. Say: "We're breathing together. You're not alone."
4. Repeat 3 times.
This shared silence is often more healing than words.

Journal Space for Friends

- How did I feel when my friend opened up to me?
- What am I afraid of when supporting them?
- What do I wish I could say?
- How can I take care of myself while being there for someone else?

Your Boundaries Matter Too

Helping someone heal doesn't mean:
- Becoming their therapist
- Taking on their pain alone
- Ignoring your own needs

It's okay to say:
- "I care, but I need support too."
- "Let's talk to someone together."
- "I'm here for you, but I also need a break."

You can support others without sacrificing yourself.

Support Resources to Share

Give your friend these trusted support options:
- CHILDLINE 1098 – 24/7 help
- iCall – 9152987821
- School counselor or mental health teacher

- **Trusted NGO:** Arpan, RAHI, Aarambh India
- **Cybercrime portal:** www.cybercrime.gov.in

You don't need all the answers—just the right direction.

Quick "Ally" Checklist

✔ I listened without interrupting
✔ I said "I believe you"
✔ I offered to help find support
✔ I respected their pace and feelings
✔ I also cared for my own emotional wellbeing

That's what being a true friend looks like.

Summary

In this chapter, you learned:

- How to respond when a friend shares their abuse story
- The right things to say (and what to avoid)
- Why your role as a listener and ally matters
- When to speak up if your friend is in danger
- How to support others while caring for yourself too

Chapter 10

Legal Protection for Teens in India

Why Knowing the Law Matters

If you've experienced or witnessed child sexual abuse (CSA), it's normal to feel afraid of involving the police or legal system.

You might wonder:
• "Will I be blamed?"
• "Will people find out?"
• "What if I'm not believed?"

Here's the truth:
You have legal rights.
The law is designed to protect you, not punish you.

In India, the Protection of Children from Sexual Offences (POCSO) Act exists just for children and teens like you. It's meant to give you safety, justice, and a child-friendly experience during the legal process.

What Is the POCSO Act?

The Protection of Children from Sexual Offences (POCSO) Act,

2012 is a special law that:
- Recognizes all forms of sexual abuse against children (under 18 years)
- Makes reporting mandatory for anyone who knows about CSA
- Ensures confidentiality and privacy
- Provides child-friendly courts and police procedures
- Punishes abusers with strict penalties
- Offers medical, legal, and psychological support for survivors

Key Terms You Should Know

Term	Meaning
Victim/Survivor	The child or teen who experienced the abuse
Accused	The person who committed the abuse
FIR	First Information Report – official complaint filed with police
CWC	Child Welfare Committee – protects your rights during the case
Special Court	A court trained to handle POCSO cases in a child-sensitive way
Support Person	Someone (often from a child rights NGO) who helps you during the legal process

Your Rights Under POCSO

You have the right to:

✔ Be heard and believed

✔ File a complaint without needing permission from an adult

✔ Keep your identity confidential

✔ Be accompanied by a parent, guardian, or support person
✔ Give your statement in a safe, non-threatening environment
✔ Be protected from the accused
✔ Medical help and therapy if needed
✔ Free legal aid
✔ Ask for speedy trial in a Special Court

What Happens If You Decide to Report?

Step-by-Step:

1. Go to a police station or call 1098 or 112 (emergency)
2. Tell what happened – you can be accompanied by a trusted adult
3. An FIR is filed
4. You may be taken for a medical check-up (only if needed)
5. Your statement is recorded in a child-friendly way (often by a female officer)
6. Police investigate, gather evidence
7. Case goes to a Special POCSO Court
8. You appear with support, and testimony may be recorded privately
9. Court decides punishment if the accused is found guilty

Remember: The law is on your side.

Will I Be Punished for Speaking Up?

Absolutely not.

You are never punished for:

- Reporting abuse
- Being scared or confused
- Not reporting immediately
- Being unsure about what happened
- Talking about someone close (even if they're a family member)

The law does not blame victims.
You have nothing to fear when asking for help.

What If I Don't Want to Go to Court?

That's understandable. It's scary to imagine.

But the system is improving:
• Many Special Courts allow video testimony
• You may sit in private chambers, not open courtrooms
• You can have a support person with you at all times
• You don't have to see the abuser face-to-face
If something feels unsafe or uncomfortable, you can ask for changes.

Who Will Support Me Legally?

These people are here for you:
• Police (trained under POCSO)
• Child Welfare Committee (CWC)
• Support Person (from NGOs or District Child Protection Unit)
• Child Psychologist or counselor
• Legal Aid Advocate (free lawyer for child victims)
You are never alone in the system.

Calming Corner: Grounding Before Testimony

Before giving a statement or going to court, try this:
"Peace in My Palm"

• **Press your thumb to each finger and say:**
  - **Thumb:** I am brave
  - **Index:** I have support
  - **Middle:** I speak my truth
  - **Ring:** I deserve justice
  - **Little:** I am healing

Breathe slowly. Repeat 2–3 times.

My Journal Space

- What questions do I have about the legal process?
- What do I fear most—and why?
- What would justice look like to me?
- What would I tell another teen scared to speak up?

FAQ – Teens and the Law

Can I report without my parents?
Yes. You can file a report on your own under POCSO.

Will I have to go on TV or in the newspaper?
No. The media is not allowed to reveal your identity.

What if I'm not sure about the details?
That's okay. Say what you remember. You are still valid.

Can I stop the case later?
Once a case is filed under POCSO, it continues in the interest of your safety and justice—but your comfort is always prioritized.

Summary

In this chapter, you learned:

- What the POCSO Act is and how it protects children and teens
- How to report abuse and what happens afterward
- What your legal rights are during the process
- That you will never be punished for speaking up
- That you are supported by a whole system of trained professionals

Chapter 11

My Body, My Rules

Owning Your Body, Owning Your Power

From the time you're little, people tell you what to wear, how to sit, who to hug. But as you grow older, one truth becomes very important: Your body belongs to YOU. Not to your family, friends, partner, or anyone else.

You have the right to say:
• "No, I don't want to be touched."
• "I need space."
• "That makes me uncomfortable."
This chapter is all about learning how to understand, protect, and express your body boundaries with confidence.

What Is Consent?

Consent means giving permission for something to happen. But not just any kind of permission—it must be:

Condition	What It Means
Freely given	You say "yes" without pressure or fear
Reversible	You can change your mind at any time
Informed	You know exactly what you're agreeing to
Enthusiastic	You feel good and excited about it—not confused or scared
Specific	Saying "yes" to a hug is not "yes" to something more

That's what healthy consent looks like.
And guess what? Silence is NOT consent. Fear is NOT consent. Guilt is NOT consent.

Touching Rules – Understanding Safe, Unsafe, and Confusing Touch

Not all touch is bad. Some touches feel good, like a parent's hug or a friend's high-five. But some touches make you freeze, feel scared, or confused.

Safe Touch:

- Feels respectful and wanted
- Happens in public spaces
- Makes you feel cared for
- You can say "no" at any time

Unsafe Touch:

- Makes you feel scared or uncomfortable
- Happens in secret or private
- Touches private parts without reason or permission
- You're told to keep it a secret

Confusing Touch:

• Seems like affection but doesn't feel right
• Comes from someone you trust, like a family member or teacher
• You're unsure whether to speak up

If it makes you feel weird inside—that's your body saying, "This isn't right."

The "Private Parts Rule"

Private parts are the areas covered by your underclothes—chest, genitals, and buttocks.

No one has the right to touch, look at, or ask you to touch their private parts.

The only exception is:

• A doctor, during a medical check-up, with your permission and a trusted adult present

The Power of "No"

Saying "NO" is not rude. It's your right.

You can say no to:

• Hugs or kisses
• Jokes or comments about your body
• Physical closeness
• Online requests for photos
• Any kind of sexual behavior

You don't owe anyone your body—not even someone you care about.

Real Voices

"I used to feel guilty saying no to hugs from relatives. But my counselor taught me: If I'm uncomfortable, I don't have to explain

why. I just have to honor how I feel."
— **Kabir, 15**
"A boy at school kept trying to touch my hair and hold my hand. Everyone said he was flirting. I didn't like it. I told him to stop. That was me taking my power back."
— **Ananya, 16**

Building Body Boundaries

Think of your body like a house. You get to decide who comes in.

Your body rules can sound like:
- "I'm not okay with hugging right now."
- "Please don't touch me."
- "I need more space."
- "I don't like that joke."

People who respect you will respect your boundaries.
People who don't? That's a red flag.

Online Boundaries Matter Too

In the digital world, body boundaries look like:
- Refusing to send photos or videos
- Saying no to inappropriate DMs
- Blocking and reporting anyone who crosses the line
- Not feeling guilty for protecting your space

Remember: Screens are not shields. Respect and consent apply online, too.

My Journal Space

- What touches make me feel safe?
- When was a time I wanted to say no but didn't?
- What does my "safe space" look like?

• What do I want others to understand about my boundaries?

Calming Corner: Personal Power Pose

Try this when you feel small or unsure:

1. Stand tall
2. Feet shoulder-width apart
3. Hands on hips
4. Breathe in confidence

5. Say aloud:

o "My body, my rules."
o "I have the right to say no."
o "I am allowed to protect myself."

This body pose activates courage.

Respect Goes Both Ways

While it's important to set your boundaries, it's also important to:

• Respect others when they say no
• Ask for permission before touching or joking
• Never pressure or guilt someone into something
• Understand that consent is about mutual comfort

Healthy friendships and relationships are based on mutual respect.

"My Rules" Checklist

✔ I don't have to accept touch I don't like
✔ I can speak up if something feels wrong
✔ I don't owe anyone access to my body
✔ I don't have to feel guilty for saying no
✔ My voice matters
✔ I respect other people's space and consent too

Summary

In this chapter, you learned:

- That your body belongs to YOU
- What consent really means (FREES)
- How to tell the difference between safe, unsafe, and confusing touch
- That saying no is your right—not your shame
- How to build boundaries that protect and empower you

Chapter 12

Everyday Empowerment

Empowerment Starts With You

You've come a long way through this book. You've faced tough truths, learned your rights, understood your body, and discovered the importance of healing. Now, **let's talk about the next step:**

How to feel strong, safe, and confident—every single day.

Empowerment is not just about fighting back.

It's about walking into a room knowing:
- "I matter."
- "I deserve respect."
- "I can trust my voice."

This chapter is about practical ways to stay safe and feel powerful—in your body, in your relationships, and in your everyday life.

What Is Everyday Empowerment?

Everyday empowerment means:
• Setting boundaries without fear
• Knowing your strengths
• Choosing people and places that make you feel safe
• Speaking up when something feels wrong
• Building habits that protect your mental and physical wellbeing
It's not about being perfect.

It's about being aware, confident, and kind to yourself.

Your Personal Safety Foundation

3 Golden Rules:
1. Trust your gut. If something feels wrong—it probably is.
2. Speak your boundaries. You don't owe silence to anyone.
3. Stay connected. Safe friendships = stronger self.
You don't need to be loud to be powerful.
Even quiet confidence is strong.

Building Body Boundaries (Every Day)

Let's turn boundary-setting into a habit.

Practice saying:
• "That makes me uncomfortable."
• "I'd prefer not to be hugged."
• "Let's not joke about my body."
• "Please don't touch my things."

Write your own list of phrases that feel natural to you.
Practice them in front of a mirror. Repeat until they feel normal.
Boundaries are not walls—they're filters to protect your peace.

Self-Trust Rituals

Create daily habits that strengthen your sense of self.

Ideas:

- **Start your day with an affirmation:** "I am strong. I am safe."
- **Check in with your feelings:** "What do I need today?"
- Use your journal to release stress
- Choose clothing that makes you feel comfortable—not anyone else
- Spend time with people who respect your voice

Affirmations for Everyday Power

Write these on sticky notes. Place them on your mirror or notebook.

- "I listen to my gut—it protects me."
- "My voice deserves to be heard."
- "Saying no is brave."
- "I can trust myself."
- "I am healing, growing, and powerful."

Repeat. Believe. Become.

My "Circle of Safety"

Who's in your safe circle?

Draw a circle. Inside it, write:

- Names of people who make you feel safe (family, friends, mentors)
- Places that bring you calm (library, classroom, home)
- Tools that support you (therapy, music, journaling)

Outside the circle, write people or things that cause stress or cross boundaries.

This exercise helps you understand who and what supports your empowerment.

Healthy Friendships and Relationships

You deserve relationships that:
• Respect your NO
• Don't pressure you to do things you're uncomfortable with
• Communicate honestly
• Uplift your self-worth
• Listen without judgment

Red flags to watch for:
Jealousy, controlling behavior
Touching you without permission
Shaming your choices
Guilting you into silence
Isolating you from others
Love doesn't hurt, scare, or silence.
Real love empowers.

Empowerment in the Digital World

You have digital rights too.

Set your online boundaries:
• Keep your profiles private
• Don't respond to creepy or sexual messages—block and report
• Never send photos or videos if you feel unsure
• Mute or unfollow anyone who disrespects your space
• Use two-factor authentication for all accounts
Say to yourself: "My digital safety matters."

Coping Tools for Bad Days

Even empowered people have rough days. When that happens:
• Take 10 deep belly breaths
• Write "I'm feeling ___ because ___"

- Go for a walk or stretch
- Talk to someone you trust
- Listen to calming music or nature sounds
- Do a simple body scan: "Where do I feel tense? Can I

breathe into that spot?"

Bad days don't erase your progress.
They remind you to rest, not quit.

My Journal Space

- What empowers me?
- Who in my life makes me feel strong and safe?
- What boundary have I set recently that I'm proud of?
- What are three qualities I love about myself?

Everyday Empowerment Toolkit

Tool	How It Helps
Daily affirmation	Builds self-trust
Personal mantra	Calms and centers your mind
Body boundary phrases	Protects your space
Trusted adult list	Keeps support close
Journaling or art	Releases heavy emotions
Circle of safety	Reminds you that you are not alone

Calming Corner: "Shield of Light" Visualization

Close your eyes.
Imagine a glowing light forming a shield around you.
It protects you from harm, disrespect, and fear.
Inside the shield, you are safe, powerful, and calm.

Breathe in: "I am strong."
Breathe out: "I release fear."

Summary

In this chapter, you learned:

- What everyday empowerment looks like
- How to build body boundaries and emotional confidence
- Tools and phrases to stay safe, calm, and clear
- That you are worthy of healthy relationships and digital safety
- That empowerment is a habit—not a one-time event

Glossary Of Important Terms

Term	Definition
Abuse	Any behavior that causes harm or violates someone's boundaries—emotionally, physically, or sexually.
Body Boundaries	Personal rules about how you want your body to be treated by others.
Consent	Giving clear, informed, and enthusiastic permission. Consent must be voluntary, and it can be withdrawn at any time.
CSA (Child Sexual Abuse)	Any sexual act involving a minor (under 18), including touching, exposure, online abuse, or manipulation.
Dissociation	A mental response to trauma where a person feels numb, disconnected from their body or surroundings.
Empowerment	Gaining strength, confidence, and control over your body, choices, and life.
Flashback	A sudden, intense memory or feeling that brings back traumatic events as if they're happening again.
Grooming	The process an abuser uses to build trust with a child or teen to eventually abuse them. This can include gifts, flattery, or manipulation.
Helpline	A phone number or chat service that offers support, counseling, or emergency aid. In India, CHILDLINE is 1098.

POCSO Act	Protection of Children from Sexual Offences Act (2012) – a special Indian law that protects children from sexual abuse.
Sextortion	A form of online abuse where someone threatens to leak private or sexual content unless demands are met.
Support Person	A trained adult who accompanies a child survivor through police and court processes.
Survivor	Someone who has experienced abuse and is on a journey of recovery and healing.
Therapy	A professional process where a counselor or psychologist helps you understand, process, and heal from difficult emotions or trauma.
Trauma	Emotional and psychological distress caused by experiencing something frightening, painful, or deeply upsetting.
Trigger	A sound, smell, place, or memory that brings back feelings from a traumatic experience.
Unsafe Touch	Any touch that makes you feel uncomfortable, scared, or hurt—especially on private parts or when asked to keep it secret.
Trusted Adult	A person (parent, teacher, counselor, NGO worker) who listens, believes, and protects your well-being.
Well-being	Your overall mental, emotional, and physical health.